THE
Emperor's
New Clothes

A Parragon Book

Published by
Parragon Books,
Unit 13–17, Avonbridge Trading Estate,
Atlantic Road, Avonmouth, Bristol BS11 9QD

Produced by
The Templar Company plc,
Pippbrook Mill, London Road, Dorking, Surrey RH4 1JE

Designed by Mark Kingsley-Monks

Printed and bound in Italy

ISBN 0-75250-929-2

— THE —
Emperor's New Clothes

Retold by Caroline Repchuk
Illustrated by Rodney Shaw

|| •PARRAGON• ||

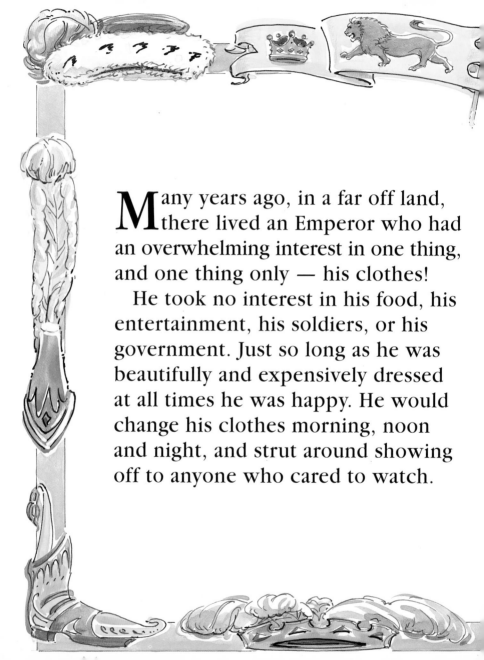

Many years ago, in a far off land, there lived an Emperor who had an overwhelming interest in one thing, and one thing only — his clothes!

He took no interest in his food, his entertainment, his soldiers, or his government. Just so long as he was beautifully and expensively dressed at all times he was happy. He would change his clothes morning, noon and night, and strut around showing off to anyone who cared to watch.

The city in which he lived was large and prosperous, and strangers often came to visit. One day two men arrived at the city gate.

They were dishonest swindlers pretending to be weavers.

"We can weave a cloth more beautiful than you could imagine," they said. "And what is more, it is magical. Only clever people can see it. Stupid people think it's invisible!"

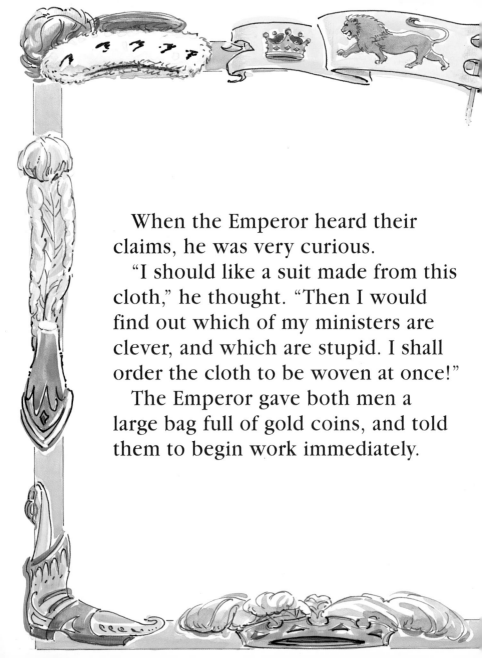

When the Emperor heard their claims, he was very curious.

"I should like a suit made from this cloth," he thought. "Then I would find out which of my ministers are clever, and which are stupid. I shall order the cloth to be woven at once!"

The Emperor gave both men a large bag full of gold coins, and told them to begin work immediately.

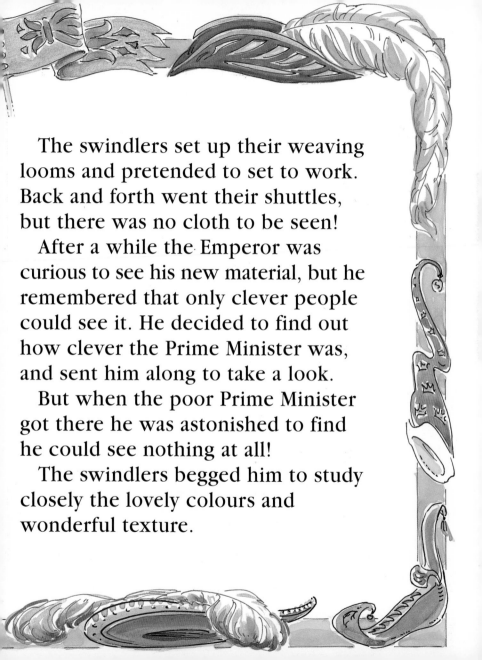

The swindlers set up their weaving looms and pretended to set to work. Back and forth went their shuttles, but there was no cloth to be seen!

After a while the Emperor was curious to see his new material, but he remembered that only clever people could see it. He decided to find out how clever the Prime Minister was, and sent him along to take a look.

But when the poor Prime Minister got there he was astonished to find he could see nothing at all!

The swindlers begged him to study closely the lovely colours and wonderful texture.

"Dear me," thought the Prime Minister to himself. "Am I stupid? I didn't think I was! No one must find out. I shall have to pretend that I can see this wonderful cloth!"

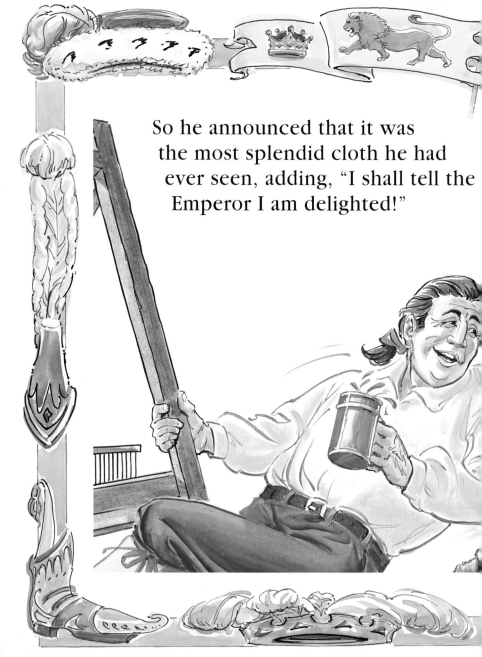

So he announced that it was the most splendid cloth he had ever seen, adding, "I shall tell the Emperor I am delighted!"

When he had gone the swindlers laughed and laughed. "We fooled him," they said.

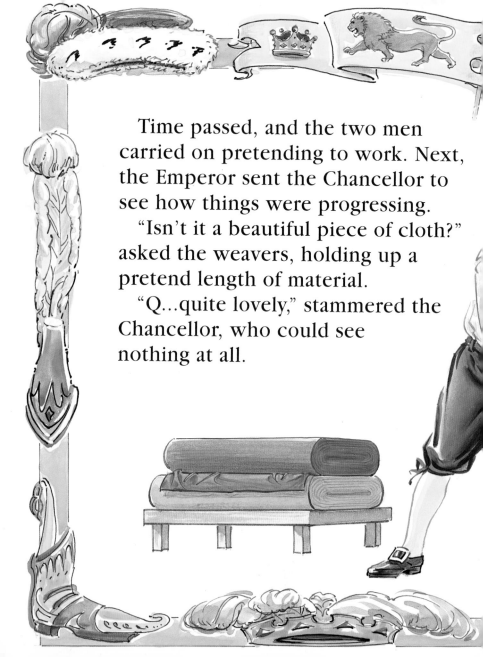

Time passed, and the two men carried on pretending to work. Next, the Emperor sent the Chancellor to see how things were progressing.

"Isn't it a beautiful piece of cloth?" asked the weavers, holding up a pretend length of material.

"Q...quite lovely," stammered the Chancellor, who could see nothing at all.

And, just like the Prime Minister, the Chancellor went back and told the Emperor that the cloth was quite superb.

The excited Emperor could wait
no longer. Off he marched to see the
material for himself, with a great
crowd of courtiers behind him.

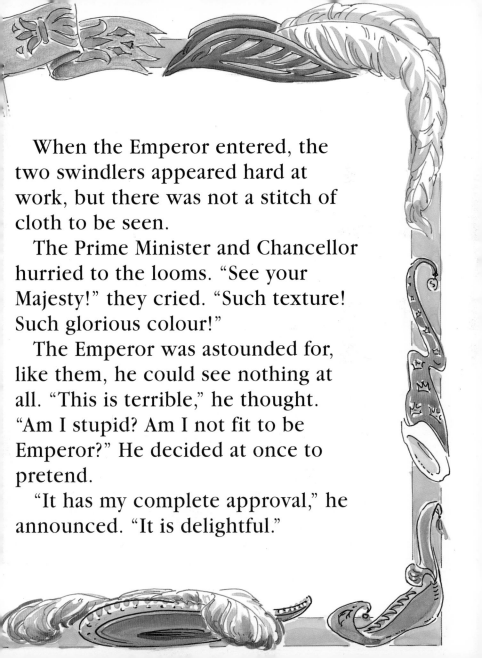

When the Emperor entered, the two swindlers appeared hard at work, but there was not a stitch of cloth to be seen.

The Prime Minister and Chancellor hurried to the looms. "See your Majesty!" they cried. "Such texture! Such glorious colour!"

The Emperor was astounded for, like them, he could see nothing at all. "This is terrible," he thought. "Am I stupid? Am I not fit to be Emperor?" He decided at once to pretend.

"It has my complete approval," he announced. "It is delightful."

His puzzled courtiers gathered round and stared. They, too, saw nothing, but no one wanted to appear stupid. "Exquisite!" they cried.

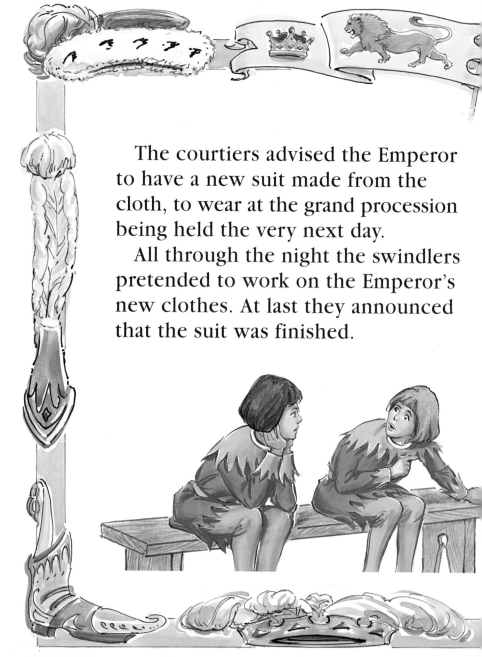

The courtiers advised the Emperor to have a new suit made from the cloth, to wear at the grand procession being held the very next day.

All through the night the swindlers pretended to work on the Emperor's new clothes. At last they announced that the suit was finished.

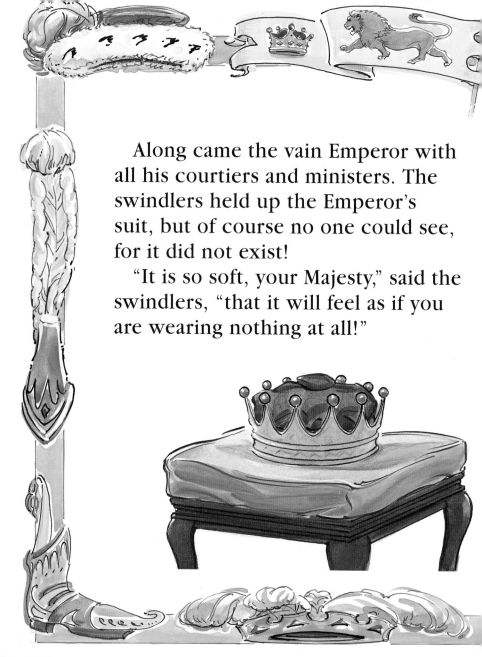

Along came the vain Emperor with all his courtiers and ministers. The swindlers held up the Emperor's suit, but of course no one could see, for it did not exist!

"It is so soft, your Majesty," said the swindlers, "that it will feel as if you are wearing nothing at all!"

The Emperor was eager to try it on and hurriedly took off all his clothes. The swindlers pretended to dress him in his fine new clothes.

The Emperor turned this way and that in front of the mirror, admiring his fine new suit.

"What a perfect fit!" exclaimed his courtiers. "It is indeed a gorgeous suit!"

"I must confess," said the Emperor, "that I look very grand indeed!" And all the time he was really wearing nothing at all!

At last it was time for the procession to begin. Two chamberlains pretended to lift the train of the cloak, and solemnly followed the Emperor out of the room.

In no time the swindlers packed their things, grabbed their bags of gold and fled from the city!

Outside in the bright sun the Emperor walked in a dignified and stately fashion at the head of the grand procession, and all the people stared as he slowly marched by.

To their amazement they could see that he was not wearing a stitch of clothing! But no one dared to admit it for fear of being thought stupid.

"What a marvellous suit!" they cried.

But one little boy could hardly believe his eyes, and suddenly he piped up, "But the Emperor has nothing on!"

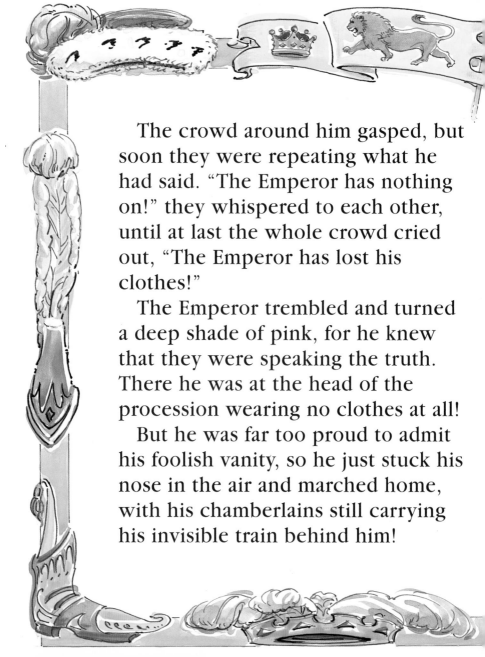

The crowd around him gasped, but soon they were repeating what he had said. "The Emperor has nothing on!" they whispered to each other, until at last the whole crowd cried out, "The Emperor has lost his clothes!"

The Emperor trembled and turned a deep shade of pink, for he knew that they were speaking the truth. There he was at the head of the procession wearing no clothes at all!

But he was far too proud to admit his foolish vanity, so he just stuck his nose in the air and marched home, with his chamberlains still carrying his invisible train behind him!

HANS CHRISTIAN ANDERSEN

Hans Christian Andersen was born in
Odense, Denmark, on April 2nd, 1805.
His family was very poor and throughout his
life he suffered much unhappiness.
Even after he had found success as a writer,
Andersen felt something of an outsider, an
aspect which often emerged in his stories.
The Emperor's New Clothes is an
unforgettable story enjoyed by every child,
but Andersen would also have enjoyed
the chance it gave him to make fun of the
rigid class system and the hypocrisy of his
own time. His world-famous fairy tales
include *The Snow Queen*, *The Little
Mermaid* and *The Ugly Duckling*, and are
amongst the most frequently translated
works of literature.
He died in 1875.